HarperCollins®, ☖®, and HarperEntertainment™ are trademarks of HarperCollins Publishers.

The Land Before Time: The Spooky Nighttime Adventure
The Land Before Time and related characters are trademarks and copyrights of Universal Studios and U-Drive Productions, Inc.
Licensed by Universal Studios Licensing LLLP. All rights reserved.

Printed in the United States of America.

Library of Congress catalog card number: 2008920012
ISBN 978-0-06-135298-0
Typography by Rick Farley and Sean Boggs
❖
First Edition

The Spooky Nighttime Adventure

Adapted by Jennifer Frantz
Illustrated by Artful Doodlers
Based on the teleplay by Jack Monaco

HarperEntertainment
An Imprint of HarperCollinsPublishers

As Petrie finished telling his scary story, he looked up to see his friends gasping in fear—all except Cera.

"I thought we were telling *scary* stories," Cera said.

"I know a scary story!" Ruby said. "There's a spooky creature called the Hidden Runner, who lives in the Mysterious Beyond. He sneaks up to your sleeping place . . . AND EATS YOU!"

Petrie dived for cover, hiding his face with his wings. "What Hidden Runner look like?" he asked, peeking out.

"No one's ever gotten a good look at him," Ruby said. "Sometimes he's hidden and sometimes he's *invisible*."

"So how do you know he is there?" Ducky asked.

"Right before Hidden Runner eats you," Ruby said, "he lets out a noisy, horrible yell—A-WOO! A-WOOOO!"

Petrie jumped behind Littlefoot.

Cera just laughed. *She* wasn't scared by Ruby's story.

That night, all the children had bad dreams about Hidden Runner . . . except Cera.

The next morning, the friends gathered around to talk about their spooky dreams.

"You all had scary sleep stories, too?" Chomper asked.

"Yup-yup-yup!" Ducky said.

Cera thought her friends were just being scaredy-eggs.

"You'd understand what's so scary if you had sleep stories too, Cera," Littlefoot said.

"Three-horns don't have sleep stories," Cera said. "Even if we did, they wouldn't scare me."

The friends decided to talk to Mr. Thicknose about Hidden Runner. Mr. Thicknose knew everything.

"Hidden Runner?" Mr. Thicknose said. "He goes from place to place and never stays long, but sometimes he comes back."

"Sometime *now?*" Petrie cried.

"Must be," Mr. Thicknose said. "And I'm finally going to see him for myself!"

Soon Mr. Thicknose and the children were off on an exciting adventure—to find Hidden Runner!

"Look out for big footprints," Mr. Thicknose said.

Petrie stared nervously into the dark woods.

"You hatchlings worry too much," Cera said. "There's nothing to be scared of."

That night, the group stopped to sleep in a clearing.

Ducky, Spike, Chomper, and Petrie tried to stay awake. They were afraid of scary sleep stories and a visit from Hidden Runner.

"Being scared is for scaredy-eggs," Cera said as she went off to bed. After all, three-horns didn't have sleep stories.

But that night, Cera *did* have a scary sleep story! In her dream, she was being chased by Hidden Runner. Suddenly the monster was gone and her friends were there.

"You're afraid, aren't you, Cera," Littlefoot teased.

"Cera is a scaredy-egg!" the others said.

"I am not!" Cera shouted, waking herself up.
She looked around the clearing and saw her friends.
"Were you having a sleep story?" Littlefoot asked.
"No," Cera said. "You just woke me up is all."
She didn't want the others to know she'd had a scary sleep story and was feeling afraid.

Suddenly, the children heard a loud noise.
A-WOO! A-WOOOO!
"What was that?" Cera asked nervously.
"Hidden Runner!" said Mr. Thicknose.

Mr. Thicknose led the group up a twisty path to the edge of a spooky cave. "Footprints!" he said. "Let's follow them."

"*Inside the cave?*" Cera said.

"You're not afraid, are you, Cera?" Littlefoot asked.

"C'mon," Ruby said. "We won't find Hidden Runner if we don't look for him."

Inside the cave, Cera tried to be brave.
  Suddenly, a huge shadow appeared out of nowhere. Then they heard Hidden Runner's loud call, *A-WOO! A-WOOOO!*

"He's gonna eat us!" Cera screamed, running outside.
In an instant, Hidden Runner's huge shadow disappeared.
"Maybe we can still catch him," Mr. Thicknose said.
"First we need to find Cera," said Littlefoot.

The group found her hiding behind a bush and looking sad.
"It's my fault you didn't get to see Hidden Runner," she said. "I'm just a big scaredy-egg."

"Being afraid doesn't mean you can't be brave, too," said Mr. Thicknose. "True bravery is admitting you're afraid and facing your fear."

Mr. Thicknose was right. Cera looked up. Then she saw something—a pair of eyes! It was Hidden Runner!

A-WOO! A-WOOOO! Hidden Runner called, then froze as he saw the group.

"He's real!" said Chomper.

"And I'm looking right at him!" said Mr. Thicknose.

Cera was still scared, but she gathered her courage. "Hi," she said. "I'm Cera."

Hidden Runner squawked. In a flash, he was gone!

"He disappeared!" said Ducky.

"Look!" Ruby said. "He doesn't disappear—he blends in!"

Everyone saw Hidden Runner step out from the trees and become visible again.

On the way home everyone talked about Hidden Runner. Cera was glad she had faced her fears and was able to see such a special creature.

"To think," said Cera, "he was more scared of us!"

Suddenly there was a loud noise from the woods behind them.

"What that?!" asked Petrie, diving for cover.

"There's always something for Petrie to be scared of!"
Littlefoot said.

"That very true," Petrie said, with a shy smile.

Everyone laughed, including Cera, who couldn't wait to get
home and tell everyone about her spooky adventure.